The
Tiara
Club

D1375351

For Princess Emily of Edinburgh,
with much love,
VF

For the little princesses Abi, Georgie,
Joesie, Tabi, Imi and Freya
SG

www.tiaraclub.co.uk

ORCHARD BOOKS
338 Euston Road, London NW1 3BH
Orchard Books Australia
Hachette Children's Books
Level 17/207 Kent Street, Sydney, NSW 2000, Australia
A Paperback Original
First published in Great Britain in 2005
Text © copyright Vivian French 2005
Illustrations © copyright Sarah Gibb 2005
The rights of Vivian French and Sarah Gibb to be
identified as the author and illustrator of this work
have been asserted by them in accordance with
the Copyright, Designs and Patents Act, 1988.

A CIP catalogue record for this book is available
from the British Library.
ISBN 1 84362 859 7
5 7 9 10 8 6 4

Printed in Great Britain

The Tiara Club

Princess Emily
and the Beautiful Fairy

By Vivian French
Illustrated by Sarah Gibb

ORCHARD BOOKS

The Royal Palace Academy
for the Preparation of Perfect Princesses

(Known to our students as '*The Princess Academy*')

OUR SCHOOL MOTTO:
A Perfect Princess always thinks of others before herself,
and is kind, caring and truthful.

We offer the complete curriculum for all princesses, including –

How to talk to a Dragon	*Designing and Creating the Perfect Ball Gown*
Creative Cooking for Perfect Palace Parties	*Avoiding Magical Mistakes*
Wishes, and how to use them Wisely	*Descending a Staircase as if Floating on Air*

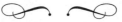

Our head teacher, Queen Gloriana, is present at all times, and students are well looked after by the school Fairy Godmother.

Visiting tutors and experts include –

KING PERCIVAL *(Dragons)*	*QUEEN MOTHER MATILDA* *(Etiquette, Posture and Poise)*
LADY VICTORIA *(Banquets)*	*THE GRAND HIGH DUCHESS DELIA (Costume)*

We award tiara points to encourage
our princesses towards the next level.
All princesses who win enough points in their
first year are welcomed to the Tiara Club
and presented with a silver tiara.

Tiara Club princesses are invited to return
next year to Silver Towers, our very special
residence for Perfect Princesses, where
they may continue their education
at a higher level.

PLEASE NOTE:
Princesses are expected to arrive at the Academy
with a *minimum* of:

TWENTY BALL GOWNS
(with all necessary hoops,
petticoats, etc)

TWELVE DAY DRESSES

SEVEN GOWNS
suitable for garden parties,
and other special
day occasions

TWELVE TIARAS

DANCING SHOES
five pairs

VELVET SLIPPERS
three pairs

RIDING BOOTS
two pairs

Cloaks, muffs, stoles, gloves
and other essential
accessories as required

Hi there! I'm Princess Emily — one of the
Rose Room princesses at the Princess
Academy. Do you know Alice and Katie
and Daisy and Charlotte and Sophia?
They're my best friends — just like you!
And have you met Princess Perfecta yet?
She's HORRID. Alice says it's because
Queen Gloriana (our head teacher) made
her repeat her first year — she didn't
get enough tiara points to get into
the Tiara Club!

Ooooh...just thinking about it
makes me shivery. It would be so
DREADFUL to have to start all over
again. Can you IMAGINE it?
Oh nooooooo!

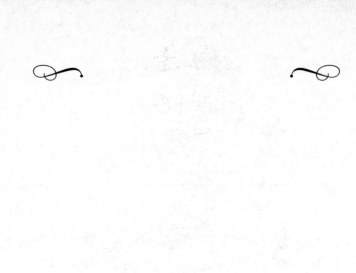

Chapter One

Do you ever feel as if a Big Black Cloud is hanging over your head? Well, the day after my birthday was like that. Isn't that awful? Even though my parents had sent me the most completely GLORIOUS pearly pink dress and a PERFECT matching tiara, I couldn't feel excited.

All of us in Rose Room had been worrying for weeks about what we were going to wear for the end of term Grand Assembly, so it was LOVELY of my parents to send me something so utterly gorgeous – but it meant I'd be different from my very best friends. That made me feel

TERRIBLE! They'd all raved about my beautiful birthday gown, of course, but I knew that secretly it MUST have made them feel worse.

I'd opened my parcel at breakfast, and I couldn't help noticing the tiny pause before they told me how lovely it was.

And then Perfecta said in a REALLY nasty voice, "Who's going to be the biggest show-off on Saturday, then?" and Floreen said, "SOME people are just SPOILT!"

But that wasn't the only reason why I had a Big Black Cloud. I was worried about my tiara points. Honestly – I was worried sick.

"I just KNOW I'm going to be here in first year for ever and ever and EVER," I said as I stood staring out of the recreation room window.

"Me too," Katie sighed. She came to stand beside me. "I got five minus points yesterday. I went down to the stable to see the ponies that pull the silver coach, and I forgot to wipe my boots when I came back in.

Queen Mum Mattie gave me a HORRIBLE row."

"You did have loads of straw in your hair as well," Sophia pointed out.

"AND you pinched all the sugar lumps from the tea trolley," Alice said. "Perfecta was FURIOUS!"

"Serves her right," said Charlotte. She gave me a comforting smile. "Do stop worrying, Emily. You must have more tiara points than Perfecta and Floreen."

"But do any of us have enough to join the Tiara Club?" Daisy asked. Nobody answered.

We couldn't, because we really and truly had no idea. We were meant to write our tiara points in our homework diaries, but we were ALWAYS forgetting!

And even when we DID remember we added them up all wrong. (Especially me.) Up until now we'd just hoped for the best, but all of a sudden it was SERIOUS! The Grand Assembly was the most important day of our lives, because that's the day when we'd find out if we'd won our places in the Tiara Club. And it was ONLY TWO DAYS AWAY!!!!! It was SO scary!!!!

"Maybe," Alice said hopefully, "we could ask Fairy G how many points we've got?"

Charlotte made a face. "She won't say. I asked her the other week."

"She just said Perfect Princesses shouldn't need to worry," Katie sighed.

"What if we asked if we need to do just a LITTLE bit better, or a LOT better?" I suggested.

Daisy shook her head. "We can't! She's in bed with a horrible cold."

"Can't she magic it away?" I asked.

"I don't think she can use magic on herself," Sophia said. "She can only—"

CRASH!!!

The recreation room door FLUNG open, and Princess Jemima came zooming in, her eyes WIDE.

"Have you HEARD?" she gasped. "Fairy G's going away!"

We stared at her.

"What do you mean?" I asked.

"She's been so poorly that Queen Gloriana's sending her off to stay with one of her sisters!

Fairy G's sisters, that is, not Queen Gloriana's. And we've got a supply teacher instead and she's called Fairy Angora!" Jemima stopped to take a breath. "Queen Gloriana says we've all got to go to the Great Hall to meet her so you've got to come NOW!" And she shot off again at high speed.

We looked at each other in astonishment. Apart from Queen Gloriana, Fairy G is MUCH the most important person at the Princess Academy. She's the one who looks after us, and tucks us up in bed at night. She teaches loads of lessons as well. She's really good fun, even if she does swell up HUGELY when she's angry! Queen Gloriana is OK, but she IS a bit scary.

I don't know about the others, but I felt quite wobbly. It was a bit like when I'm at home and my mum has to go off for a royal tour, and I get left behind.

"I DO hope she gets better soon," I said. Charlotte nodded.

"Do you think she'll be better by the end of term?" Sophia asked.

"If she isn't," Daisy said, "who'll tell us about our tiara points?"

Alice shrugged. "Queen Gloriana, I should think. Come on! Let's go and check out – what was her name?"

"Fairy Angora," Katie said, and we trooped out of the recreation room and along the black and white marble corridor that leads to the Great Hall. As we came through the door Queen Gloriana was walking onto the stage, and beside her was the most BEAUTIFUL fairy!

Chapter Two

I don't think any of us heard what Queen Gloriana said for at least the first two minutes. We were all too busy staring. Fairy Angora was SO lovely, and her dress was totally AMAZING. It was made of some strange floaty material, and it kept changing colour.

First it was soft pink, and then palest blue...and then it drifted back to pink again. I suddenly realised Queen Gloriana was still talking.

"...and SO, Princesses," she said, "as the Fairy Godmother Agency is EXTREMELY short staffed, Fairy Angora has agreed to come, even though she has not yet quite completed her training. And now, please give Fairy Angora a HUGE welcome to the Princess Academy!"

Of course we all clapped wildly. As we moved out of the Great Hall there was a MASSIVE buzz of excitement. Fairy G usually took the next lesson (*How to Avoid Magical Mistakes*) so maybe we'd have Fairy Angora instead!

We practically ran to the classroom. As we pulled out our chairs there was a tinkling noise, and Fairy Angora floated in.

"Ooooooh," she said, and her voice was small and sweet and whispery. "Aren't you all the sweetest little darlings?

Now, what shall we do first?" She looked round our classroom. "Oh dear. SO boring! Shall we make this a PRETTY room?" And she waved her wand. Silver sparkles flew in all directions – and the next minute there were roses EVERYWHERE!

Perfecta put up her hand. "Excuse me," she said, "but that was FANTASTIC! What else can you do?"

Fairy Angora went pink and fluttery. "Oh – quite a lot of things, really. Of course, I haven't got as far as Pumpkins and Coaches. That's next term."

Perfecta smiled a hugely false smile. "So," she said, "do you know about wishes?"

"Oh YES!" Fairy Angora beamed. "I know ALL about wishes!"

And then – would you believe it? Perfecta burst into absolute floods of tears, and sobbed, "That's so WONDERFUL! Please please PLEASE can I have a wish? I've got NOTHING to wear for the Grand Assembly!"

Princess Perfecta is VERY clever. We all knew she wasn't really crying, but enormous tears streamed down her cheeks as she gazed imploringly at Fairy Angora.

Fairy Angora hesitated.

"Well..." she said slowly. "I'm not REALLY supposed to GIVE wishes, because I don't have my final certificate."

"Boo hoo HOOOOOOOOO!" Perfecta threw herself onto the floor. "I'll be the ONLY princess wearing tatters and rags..."

"No you won't!" Sophia snapped. "We've NONE of us got anything special to wear!"

"Emily has! She's got the most BEAUTIFUL new dress! AND a sparkly new tiara!" Perfecta wailed. "DEAR Fairy Angora, you look SO kind...PLEASE help me!"

Fairy Angora was looking very upset herself. "You poor girl," she said. "Maybe it would be all right if I gave you just a LITTLE wish..."

Of course, Perfecta stopped crying at once. She sat bolt upright. "I'd like a dress," she said. "A dress like Emily's!"

Fairy Angora's wand really was very sparkly! MUCH more than Fairy G's. And it glowed a beautiful forget-me-not blue as she waved it...

TINGLE...PING!!!!!!!!!!

The dress was EXACTLY like mine! I couldn't say anything, though, because suddenly everybody was asking for wishes. Honestly, I couldn't hear myself THINK!

Fairy Angora began to look a bit flustered. "Oh dear!" she said. "I really shouldn't – I mean, I can't—"

"But it won't be FAIR if we

don't ALL have wishes!'
Ermentrude thumped her fist on
the table.

"NO," Floreen whined. "It
won't!"

Poor Fairy Angora went very
pale. "I'll see what I can do,"
she said. "Only PLEASE don't all
talk at once!"

I felt SO sorry for her. She looked as if she was about to burst into tears herself.

"Why don't we ask in turn," I suggested.

Fairy Angora gulped. "Who's first?" she asked.

Floreen wanted a tiara just like mine. Lisa chose a new dress, and so did Jemima, and then everybody wanted dresses, except for Nancy. She asked for a tiara decorated with silver butterflies.

Fairy Angora looked more and more anxious as the dresses piled higher and higher, and I suddenly wondered if the magic was wearing out. Her wand had ALMOST stopped sparkling, and was a funny pale yellow colour. Then Freya's dress came out blue instead of pink, and Jemima had spots instead of bows!

"Ask for something easy,"
I whispered when at last it came
to our turn.

Charlotte asked for curly hair.
Katie asked for new shoes, and
Daisy for a feather boa. Sophia
asked for a silk shawl, and Alice
wanted sparkly socks.

I was last, and I couldn't think of anything. Honestly, I couldn't. The only thing I really wanted was tiara points, and it would have been SO cheating to ask for those. In the end I asked for a powder puff.

Fairy Angora waved her wand for the last time. One single silver sparkle floated into the air, and then—

TINGLE...PLUNK!

There was my powder puff, AND a pot of sparkly powder. It was SO pretty!

Charlotte began to clap, and everyone joined in – even Perfecta and Floreen. Fairy Angora looked a little bit brighter. "I DO hope you enjoy your wishes," she said. "Oh, maybe you should take your dresses and hang them up?"

At once there was a dash for the door...and I noticed something weird.

Do you remember I told you Nancy wanted a tiara with butterflies on it?

Well, the butterflies had turned into tiny silver caterpillars!!!

Chapter Three

"CATERPILLARS?" Alice stared at me as if she thought I was mad.

"Yes," I said.

"Emily!" Daisy waved her wonderfully fluffy new feather boa under my nose. "That's SUCH a fib!"

"They WERE," I said. "HONESTLY!"

Katie looked at me doubtfully, and bent down to tighten the straps of her new sparkly shoes. "I HATE caterpillars," she said.

Sophia shook her head. "Shouldn't you save your shoes for the Assembly?"

"I thought I'd wear them in." Katie stood up. "Don't they look FABULOUS?"

They did, but it was a good thing she'd finished fiddling with them because just then the bell rang for Deportment. We had to scurry off as fast as we could because Deportment is taken by Queen Gloriana, and she HATES it if we're late. She gives a minus tiara point for every minute we miss! And we would have just about got there in time, but Daisy's fluffy feather boa fluttered off her neck, and ZOOMED away all by itself down the corridor!

"QUICK!" Daisy yelled. "CATCH IT!"

We dashed after it as fast as we could go. Charlotte was about to catch it (she can run like the wind) when the SCARIEST voice asked, "What EXACTLY is going on?"

And as Queen Gloriana swept towards us the feather boa twitched, and disappeared round a corner.

We were each given TWENTY minus tiara points. It was utterly dreadful. I could see Perfecta and Floreen sniggering as we were sent to stand at the back of the class.

"I'm SO, SO sorry," Daisy whispered.

"Don't worry," Charlotte whispered back.

Queen Gloriana turned to see who was whispering.

"WHO—?" she began, and then she stopped.

And stared.

So did EVERYBODY.

Charlotte's hair was growing STRAIGHT UPWARDS!

Poor Charlotte couldn't see what was going on. She put her hand to her head, and gasped.

"Is this some kind of silly joke?" Queen Gloriana asked in her chilliest voice. "Because if it is, I don't think it at ALL funny. Princess Charlotte, I expected better behaviour from you. MUCH better. Take ten minus tiara points."

Charlotte burst into tears, and ran out of the room.

"PLEASE, your Majesty," I said hurriedly, "it's not Charlotte's fault! TRULY it isn't!" And I rushed after Charlotte.

I found her in the downstairs cloakroom with her head under the cold water tap. She was trying to make her hair lie down, but it wouldn't.

"I'll have to have it all cut off!"
she wailed. "Oh, I wish Fairy G
was here! SHE'D know what
to do!"

"I'll go and find Fairy Angora,"
I said, and I zipped out of the
cloakroom towards Fairy G's
study.

Fairy Angora opened the door
the minute I knocked.

"Please!" I panted. "PLEASE! Charlotte's hair just WON'T stay down, and Daisy's feather boa is whizzing about the school, and we're in SUCH trouble! PLEASE could you come and tell Queen Gloriana it SO isn't Charlotte's fault, and can you do something about her hair?"

Fairy Angora looked horrified. "But I CAN'T!" she said. "I haven't any magic left!" and she blushed. "You see, I'm still in training, so I only have one wandful of magic, and it's ALL gone." She went even redder. "I should NEVER have given you those wishes.

47

If the Fairy Godmothers' Agency EVER finds out they'll send me away. PLEASE don't tell anyone what I did!"

I couldn't believe what I was hearing.

FAIRY ANGORA COULDN'T HELP US!

My brain was whirling round and round and ROUND, and I kept thinking, just like Charlotte, I WISH FAIRY G WAS HERE!

And I had an utterly and totally BRILLIANT idea. "What would happen," I asked, "if we gave our wishes back? What if we gave back all the dresses and tiaras and my powder puff and everything? Would you be able to get the magic back into your wand?"

Fairy Angora stared at me, and then she nodded. "Yes," she said. "At least, I think so."

I didn't know how to explain the next part of my idea without sounding rude, so I just had to say it straight out.

"If you CAN get the magic back, would there be enough for one big wish? Could I wish Fairy G was all better, and back here at the Princess Academy?"

I'd thought Fairy Angora would be offended, but she wasn't. She gave a little sigh instead.

"Emily," she said, "I do wish you'd thought of that before."

"Me too," I said, and I really really REALLY meant it.

Chapter Four

That was the easy bit. The problem was how was how to get all the first year princesses to give up their lovely dresses...ESPECIALLY Perfecta and Floreen!

Charlotte, Alice, Katie, Daisy and Sophia did their best to help, but it took us AGES.

Luckily nearly everyone loves Fairy G. When we explained we needed the dresses to get the magic back so Fairy Angora could make her better, they sighed a bit, then stomped off to fetch them. Nancy was MORE than happy to give us back her caterpillar tiara. She said it was creepy.

But we were left with three HUGE problems, and we didn't know WHAT to do.

Perfecta absolutely WOULDN'T give up her dress.

Floreen totally WOULDN'T give up her tiara.

And WE kept getting minus tiara points.

Charlotte's hair settled down, but Daisy's boa kept popping up in the MOST awkward places.

She got more and MORE minus tiara points for untidiness until FINALLY Daisy caught it – but then Queen Mum Mattie gave Daisy five minus points for running in the corridor.

Sophia woke up to find her shawl had vanished. Guess where it was? In the kitchen. Cook Clara said Sophia must have been playing with the kitchen maids, and gave her three minus points.

Katie's shoes danced off on their
own the moment she took them
off, and King Percival tripped
over them. EIGHT minus points
for Katie!

Alice's sparkly socks made her feet itch, and she got six minus points for scratching in Assembly.

We were DESPERATE. We just HAD to get Fairy G back, but HOW?

"At least we'll all be repeating the first year together," Charlotte said gloomily. "It's the Grand Assembly tomorrow, and we must have FAR more minus tiara points than plus ones."

"NO!" I said. "We'll get Fairy G back, and she'll sort it out. Let's go and see Fairy Angora after tea. We'll take her the dresses and Nancy's tiara and our things.

Maybe that'll be enough to refill the wand."

But it wasn't. Fairy Angora waved her wand over the dresses and the tiara and the wriggling boa...but nothing happened.

No sparkles. Nothing. And the wand stayed a nasty yellow.

"We need EVERYTHING," she said sadly. "I think the magic must have been at its strongest when I wished for Perfecta's dress, and Floreen's tiara."

"Oh," I said.

"I'm SO sorry." Fairy Angora put her wand down, and looked at us.

"Do you miss Fairy G VERY much?"

We nodded.

"I'd absolutely HATE it if I have to repeat the first year, but that's not the most important thing," Katie said.

"That's right," Alice agreed. "We just want Fairy G back!"

And that was when I had the best idea I'd ever EVER had.

Suddenly I knew EXACTLY how I could persuade Perfecta and Floreen to give up the dress and the tiara! I swallowed, and tried to take no notice of the fluttery feelings in my stomach.

"Excuse me!" I said. "I won't be long!" And I hurried out of Fairy G's study.

"I'VE DONE IT!" I yelled as I zoomed back through the door, the dress over my arm and the tiara clutched safely in my hand.

Sophia LEAPT to her feet.

"EMILY!" she said. "You DIDN'T give Perfecta your BEAUTIFUL birthday dress!"

I nodded, trying to look as if I didn't care one teeny tiny bit.

"It was the only way," I said. "And I gave Floreen my tiara. It doesn't matter – honestly! Besides, I want to wear an old dress for the Assembly, just like all of you."

"Oh EMILY!" Charlotte said, and she hugged me.

"And now can we try and get the magic back?" I asked Fairy Angora. She nodded as she looked at the heap of dresses and bits and pieces on the floor. Then she bit her lip, and waved her wand.

"Oh my magic wishes," she whispered. "Please – BE GONE!"

There was a MASSIVE flash, and we jumped.

The floor was clear – *AND FAIRY ANGORA'S WAND WAS BRIGHT BLUE!!!!*

"WOW!" we breathed, and Daisy whispered, "MAGIC!"

I looked anxiously at Fairy Angora. "Please!" I begged. "PLEASE wish for Fairy G to be better! PLEASE let her come back right NOW THIS MINUTE!"

Fairy Angora smiled, and waved her wand again. We held our breath.

There was a tinkling of silver bells...and for a moment the whole room was full of dancing shimmering silver sparkles...but nothing else. And Fairy Angora's wand was back to that horrid nasty yellow.

"Oh dear," she said sadly. "It didn't work."

We positively dragged ourselves out of Fairy G's study.

Chapter Five

I don't think we'd EVER felt as
DREADFUL as we did on the
morning of the Grand Assembly.
It was supposed to be the most
glorious day of the whole school
year – but for us it was the
WORST. All the other princesses
were FURIOUS with us, and
I could SO see why.

We'd taken away their truly glorious dresses – but Fairy G wasn't back!

And we had heaps and heaps and HEAPS of minus tiara points.

We held hands as we trailed miserably down the stairs.

The Great Hall was PACKED. I've NEVER seen so many Kings and Queens and Princes and

Princesses all in one place.

There was a burst of trumpets as Queen Gloriana sailed onto the stage to join Queen Mother Matilda, and Lady Victoria, and King Percival, and all the other teachers who come to the Academy.

Everyone was there except Fairy G.

"I am SO pleased to welcome you all to our end of year ceremony," Queen Gloriana announced. "We have had another excellent year, and I am happy to say that many of our princesses have won a splendid number of tiara points. Some, alas, have NOT done so well."

I felt Charlotte squeeze my hand. I tried to smile at her, but I couldn't. I blinked to stop myself crying, but a tear trickled down my nose.

Queen Gloriana was still talking. "Now, I am truly delighted to welcome our VERY special guest.

She will award all the tiara points, and she has the names of the princesses who have won their place in the Tiara Club!"

There was another HUGE fanfare of trumpets...and my mouth dropped WIDE open. Honestly – I GAWPED!

Fairy G, bigger and better than I'd ever seen her, was floating down onto the stage in a twinkly pink cloud of fairy dust. She landed with a solid THUMP! and beamed at us.

"I'M SO PLEASED TO BE HERE!" she boomed.

"I WOULD NOT HAVE BEEN
ABLE TO ATTEND, HOWEVER,
HAD IT NOT BEEN FOR THE
EFFORTS OF SIX VERY SPECIAL
PRINCESSES – THE PRINCESSES

EMILY, ALICE, CHARLOTTE, KATIE, DAISY AND SOPHIA! AND I WISH TO AWARD THEM ONE HUNDRED TIARA POINTS EACH AS A MARK OF MY APPRECIATION!"

Tantara! Tantara! Tantara! went the trumpets – and the six of us stood and STARED at each other. My heart was pitter-pattering so loudly I couldn't breathe, and a sudden wild and fantastical hope zoomed into my head!!!!

I hardly DARED to think it...but could that mean we had enough tiara points? Totally mad sums skittered in and out of my brain.

Was a hundred enough? I didn't know! Oh, if ONLY I'd counted my points – if only I'd written them down – if only, IF ONLY!!!!

Tantara! Tantara! Tantara! went the trumpets again – and my stomach fluttered with a million BILLION butterflies as I watched Fairy G hand Queen Gloriana a silver envelope.

It seemed like a hundred thousand years before Queen Gloriana pulled out the paper inside.

"Ahem," she said. "I have much pleasure in welcoming the following princesses to the

Tiara Club, *Princess Alice* (and Alice squeaked! She really did!), *Princess Daisy, Princess Sophia, Princess Katie, Princess Charlotte* and—"

Queen Gloriana paused for a second, and I nearly DIED—

"and, of course, *Princess Emily*!"

I didn't know what to do.

Nor did any of my friends.

We were STUNNED!!!

Then Charlotte dug her elbow into me. "LOOK!" she whispered.

A deep rose red carpet was rolling across the floor of the Great Hall, and it stopped right in front of us. We were trembling as we stepped onto it. Pale pink rose petals fluttered down, and I'm certain I could hear the sounds of birds singing as the invisible golden trumpets sang out yet again...and as we processed up the rose red carpet towards the waiting Queen Gloriana and Fairy G, I suddenly realised we were ALL dressed in the most beautiful BEAUTIFUL rose petal satin gowns.

We reached Queen Gloriana, and we curtsied...PERFECTLY.

"Welcome, princesses," Queen Gloriana said. "Welcome to the Tiara Club!"

And I nearly BURST with pride as I took my tiara...the tiara that meant I was a Perfect Princess – and a member of the Tiara Club!

P.S. I'll see you next term...in the Silver Towers!

Dear Princess Emily,

I PASSED! And now I'm a REAL Fairy Godmother. Thank you for everything you taught me. One day I hope some princesses will love me as much as you love Fairy G.

All VERY best wishes,

Fairy GODMOTHER

Angora xxx

Princess Emily
The Tiara Club
The Silver Towers
The Royal Palace Academy
for the Preparation of
Perfect Princesses

What happens in
Silver Towers?

Find out in

Princess Charlotte
and the **Enchanted Rose**

Princess Katie
and the **Missing Kitten**

Princess Daisy
and the **Magical Merry-Go-Round**

Princess Alice
and the **Crystal Slipper**

Princess Sophia
and the **Prince's Party**

Princess Emily
and the **Wishing Star**

Check out

The Tiara Club

website at:

www.tiaraclub.co.uk

You'll find Perfect Princess games and fun things to do, as well as news on the Tiara Club and all your favourite princesses!

Win a Tiara Club
Perfect Princess Prize!

Look for the secret word in mirror writing hidden in
a tiara in each of the Tiara Club books. Each book
has one word. Put together the six words from books
1 to 6 to make a special Perfect Princess sentence,
then send it to us. Each month, we will put the
correct entries in a draw and one lucky reader will
receive a magical Perfect Princess prize!

Send your Perfect Princess sentence, your name
and your address on a postcard to:
The Tiara Club Competition,
Orchard Books, 338 Euston Road,
London, NW1 3BH

Australian readers should write to:
Hachette Children's Books,
Level 17/207 Kent Street, Sydney, NSW 2000.

Only one entry per child.
Final draw: 31 October 2006

The Tiara Club

By Vivian French
Illustrated by Sarah Gibb

All priced at £3.99.

The Tiara Club books are available from all good bookshops,
or can be ordered direct from the publisher:
Orchard Books, PO BOX 29, Douglas IM99 1BQ.
Credit card orders please telephone 01624 836000 or fax 01624 837033
or visit our Internet site: www.wattspub.co.uk
or e-mail: bookshop@enterprise.net for details.

To order please quote title, author, ISBN and your full name and address.
Cheques and postal orders should be made payable to 'Bookpost plc.'
Postage and packing is FREE within the UK
(overseas customers should add £2.00 per book).

Prices and availability are subject to change.